Holiday Romance
In Four Parts

MAVEN BOOKS

Holiday Romance

In Four Parts

Charles Dickens

MAVEN BOOKS

Chennai   Trichy   Tirunelveli   New Delhi

MAVEN BOOKS

An Imprint of **MJP Publishers**

ISBN 978-93-87488-62-5 **Maven Books**

All rights reserved   No. 44, Nallathambi Street,
Printed and bound in India   Triplicane, Chennai 600 005

MJP 611   © Publishers, 2018

Publisher : C. Janarthanan

Publisher's Note

The legacy of a country is in its varied cultural heritage, historical literature, developments in the field of economy and science. The top nations in the world are competing in the field of science, economy and literature. This vast legacy has to be conserved and documented so that it can be bestowed to the future generation. The knowledge of this legacy is slowly getting perished in the present generation due to lack of documentation.

Keeping this in mind, the concern with retrospective acquiring of rare books has been accented recently by the burgeoning reprint industry. Maven Books is gratified to retrieve the rare collections with a view to bring back those books that were landmarks in their time.

In this effort, a series of rare books would be republished under the banner, "Maven Books". The books in the reprint series have been carefully selected for their contemporary usefulness as well as their historical importance within the intellectual. We reconstruct the book with slight enhancements made for better presentation, without affecting the contents of the original edition.

Most of the works selected for republishing covers a huge range of subjects, from history to anthropology. We believe this reprint edition will be a service to the numerous researchers and practitioners active in this fascinating field. We allow readers to experience the wonder of peering into a scholarly work of the highest order and seminal significance.

Maven Books

Contents

Part I   Introductory Romance from the Pen of William Tinkling, Esq.   1

Part II   Romance from the Pen of Miss Alice Rainbird   15

Part III   Romance from the Pen of Lieut.-Col. Robin Redforth   31

Part IV   Romance from the Pen of Miss Nettie Ashford   47

Part I

Introductory Romance from the Pen of William Tinkling, Esq.[1]

---

1.   Aged eight.

THIS beginning-part is not made out of anybody's head, you know. It's real. You must believe this beginning-part more than what comes after, else you won't understand how what comes after came to be written. You must believe it all; but you must believe this most, please. I am the editor of it. Bob Redforth (he's my cousin, and shaking the table on purpose) wanted to be the editor of it; but I said he shouldn't because he couldn't. *He* has no idea of being an editor.

Nettie Ashford is my bride. We were married in the right-hand closet in the corner of the dancing-school, where first we met, with a ring (a green one) from Wilkingwater's toy-shop. *I* owed for it out of my pocket-money. When the rapturous ceremony was over, we all four went up the lane and let off a cannon (brought loaded in Bob Redforth's waistcoat-pocket) to announce our nuptials. It flew right up when it went off, and turned over. Next day, Lieut.-Col. Robin Redforth was united, with similar ceremonies, to Alice Rainbird. This time the cannon burst with a most terrific explosion, and made a puppy bark.

My peerless bride was, at the period of which we now treat, in captivity at Miss Grimmer's. Drowvey and Grimmer is the partnership, and opinion is divided which is the greatest beast. The lovely bride of the colonel was also immured in the dungeons of the same establishment. A vow was entered into, between the colonel and myself, that we would cut them out on the following Wednesday when walking two and two.

Under the desperate circumstances of the case, the active brain of the colonel, combining with his lawless pursuit (he is a pirate), suggested an attack with fireworks. This, however, from motives of humanity, was abandoned as too expensive.

Lightly armed with a paper-knife buttoned up under his jacket, and waving the dreaded black flag at the end of a cane, the colonel took command of me at two P.M. on the eventful and appointed day. He had drawn out the plan of attack on a piece of paper, which was rolled up round a hoop-stick. He showed it to me. My position and my full-length portrait (but my real ears don't stick out horizontal) was behind a corner lamp-post, with written orders to remain there till I should see Miss Drowvey fall. The Drowvey who was to fall was the one in spectacles, not the one with the large lavender bonnet. At that signal I was to rush forth, seize my bride, and fight my way to the lane. There a junction would be effected between myself and the colonel; and putting our brides behind us, between ourselves and the palings, we were to conquer or die.

The enemy appeared,—approached. Waving his black flag, the colonel attacked. Confusion ensued. Anxiously I awaited my signal; but my signal came not. So far from falling, the hated Drowvey in spectacles appeared to me to have muffled the colonel's head in his outlawed banner, and to be pitching into him with a parasol. The one in the lavender bonnet also performed prodigies of valour with her fists on his back. Seeing that all was for the moment lost, I fought my desperate way hand to hand to the lane. Through taking the back road, I was so fortunate as to meet nobody, and arrived there uninterrupted.

It seemed an age ere the colonel joined me. He had been to the jobbing tailor's to be sewn up in several places, and attributed our defeat to the refusal of the detested Drowvey to fall. Finding her so obstinate, he had said to her, 'Die, recreant!' but had found her no more open to reason on that point than the other.

My blooming bride appeared, accompanied by the colonel's bride, at the dancing-school next day. What? Was her face averted from me? Hah? Even so. With a look of scorn, she put into my hand a bit of paper, and took another partner. On the paper was pencilled, 'Heavens! Can I write the word? Is my husband a cow?'

In the first bewilderment of my heated brain, I tried to think what slanderer could have traced my family to the ignoble animal mentioned above. Vain were my endeavours. At the end of that dance I whispered the colonel to come into the cloak-room, and I showed him the note.

'There is a syllable wanting,' said he, with a gloomy brow.

'Hah! What syllable?' was my inquiry.

'She asks, can she write the word? And no; you see she couldn't,' said the colonel, pointing out the passage.

'And the word was?' said I.

'Cow—cow—coward,' hissed the pirate-colonel in my ear, and gave me back the note.

Feeling that I must for ever tread the earth a branded boy,— person I mean,—or that I must clear up my honour, I demanded to be tried by a court-martial. The colonel admitted my right to be tried. Some difficulty was found in composing the court, on account of the Emperor of France's aunt refusing to let him come out. He was to be the president. Ere yet we had appointed a substitute, he made his escape over the back-wall, and stood among us, a free monarch.

The court was held on the grass by the pond. I recognised, in a certain admiral among my judges, my deadliest foe. A co-coa-nut had given rise to language that I could not brook; but confiding in my innocence, and also in the knowledge that the President of the United States (who sat next him) owed me a knife, I braced myself for the ordeal.

It was a solemn spectacle, that court. Two executioners with pinafores reversed led me in. Under the shade of an umbrella I perceived my bride, supported by the bride of the pirate-colonel. The president, having reproved a little female ensign for tittering, on a matter of life or death, called upon me to plead, 'Coward or no coward, guilty or not guilty?' I pleaded in a firm tone, 'No coward and not guilty.' (The little female ensign being again reproved by the president for misconduct, mutinied, left the court, and threw stones.)

My implacable enemy, the admiral, conducted the case against me. The colonel's bride was called to prove that I had remained behind the corner lamp-post during the engagement. I might have been spared the anguish of my own bride's being also made a witness to the same point, but the admiral knew where to wound me. Be still, my soul, no matter. The colonel was then brought forward with his evidence.

It was for this point that I had saved myself up, as the turning-point of my case. Shaking myself free of my guards,—who had no business to hold me, the stupids, unless I was found guilty,—I asked the colonel what he considered the first duty of a soldier? Ere he could reply, the President of the United States rose and informed the court, that my foe, the admiral, had suggested 'Bravery,' and that prompting a witness wasn't fair. The president of the court immediately ordered the admiral's mouth to be filled with leaves, and tied up with string. I had the satisfaction of seeing the sentence carried into effect before the proceedings went further.

I then took a paper from my trousers-pocket, and asked, 'What do you consider, Col. Redford, the first duty of a soldier? Is it obedience?'

'It is,' said the colonel.

'Is that paper—please to look at it—in your hand?'

'It is,' said the colonel.

'Is it a military sketch?'

'It is,' said the colonel.

'Of an engagement?'

'Quite so,' said the colonel.

'Of the late engagement?'

'Of the late engagement.'

'Please to describe it, and then hand it to the president of the court.'

From that triumphant moment my sufferings and my dangers were at an end. The court rose up and jumped, on discovering that I had strictly obeyed orders. My foe, the admiral, who though muzzled was malignant yet, contrived to suggest that I was dishonoured by having quitted the field. But the colonel himself had done as much, and gave his opinion, upon his word and honour as a pirate, that when all was lost the field might be quitted without disgrace. I was going to be found 'No coward and not guilty,' and my blooming bride was going to be publicly restored to my arms in a procession, when an unlooked-for event disturbed the general rejoicing. This was no other than the Emperor of France's aunt catching hold of his hair. The proceedings abruptly terminated, and the court tumultuously dissolved.

It was when the shades of the next evening but one were beginning to fall, ere yet the silver beams of Luna touched the earth, that four forms might have been descried slowly advancing towards the weeping willow on the borders of the pond, the now deserted scene of the day before yesterday's agonies and triumphs. On a nearer approach, and by a practised eye, these might have been identified as the forms of the pirate-colonel with his bride, and of the day before yesterday's gallant prisoner with his bride.

On the beauteous faces of the Nymphs dejection sat enthroned. All four reclined under the willow for some minutes without speaking, till at length the bride of the colonel poutingly observed, 'It's of no use pretending any more, and we had better give it up.'

'Hah!' exclaimed the pirate. 'Pretending?'

'Don't go on like that; you worry me,' returned his bride.

The lovely bride of Tinkling echoed the incredible declaration. The two warriors exchanged stony glances.

'If,' said the bride of the pirate-colonel, 'grown-up people WON'T do what they ought to do, and WILL put us out, what comes of our pretending?'

'We only get into scrapes,' said the bride of Tinkling.

'You know very well,' pursued the colonel's bride, 'that Miss Drowvey wouldn't fall. You complained of it yourself. And you know how disgracefully the court-martial ended. As to our marriage; would my people acknowledge it at home?'

'Or would my people acknowledge ours?' said the bride of Tinkling.

Again the two warriors exchanged stony glances.

'If you knocked at the door and claimed me, after you were told to go away,' said the colonel's bride, 'you would only have your hair pulled, or your ears, or your nose.'

'If you persisted in ringing at the bell and claiming me,' said the bride of Tinkling to that gentleman, 'you would have things dropped on your head from the window over the handle, or you would be played upon by the garden-engine.'

'And at your own homes,' resumed the bride of the colonel, 'it would be just as bad. You would be sent to bed, or something equally undignified. Again, how would you support us?'

The pirate-colonel replied in a courageous voice, 'By rapine!' But his bride retorted, 'Suppose the grown-up people wouldn't be rapined?' 'Then,' said the colonel, 'they should pay the penalty in blood.'—'But suppose they should object,' retorted his bride, 'and wouldn't pay the penalty in blood or anything else?'

A mournful silence ensued.

'Then do you no longer love me, Alice?' asked the colonel.

'Redforth! I am ever thine,' returned his bride.

'Then do you no longer love me, Nettie?' asked the present writer.

'Tinkling! I am ever thine,' returned my bride.

We all four embraced. Let me not be misunderstood by the giddy. The colonel embraced his own bride, and I embraced mine. But two times two make four.

'Nettie and I,' said Alice mournfully, 'have been considering our position. The grown-up people are too strong for us. They make us ridiculous. Besides, they have changed the times. William Tinkling's baby brother was christened yesterday. What took place? Was any king present? Answer, William.'

I said No, unless disguised as Great-uncle Chopper.

'Any queen?'

There had been no queen that I knew of at our house. There might have been one in the kitchen: but I didn't think so, or the servants would have mentioned it.

'Any fairies?'

None that were visible.

'We had an idea among us, I think,' said Alice, with a melancholy smile, 'we four, that Miss Grimmer would prove to be the wicked fairy, and would come in at the christening with her crutch-stick, and give the child a bad gift. Was there anything of that sort? Answer, William.'

I said that ma had said afterwards (and so she had), that Great-uncle Chopper's gift was a shabby one; but she hadn't said a bad one. She had called it shabby, electrotyped, second-hand, and below his income.

'It must be the grown-up people who have changed all this,' said Alice. 'We couldn't have changed it, if we had been so inclined, and we never should have been. Or perhaps Miss Grimmer *is* a wicked fairy after all, and won't act up to it because the grown-up people have persuaded her not to. Either way, they would make us ridiculous if we told them what we expected.'

'Tyrants!' muttered the pirate-colonel.

'Nay, my Redforth,' said Alice, 'say not so. Call not names, my Redforth, or they will apply to pa.'

'Let 'em,' said the colonel. 'I do not care. Who's he?'

Tinkling here undertook the perilous task of remonstrating with his lawless friend, who consented to withdraw the moody expressions above quoted.

'What remains for us to do?' Alice went on in her mild, wise way. 'We must educate, we must pretend in a new manner, we must wait.'

The colonel clenched his teeth,—four out in front, and a piece of another, and he had been twice dragged to the door of a dentist-despot, but had escaped from his guards. 'How educate? How pretend in a new manner? How wait?'

'Educate the grown-up people,' replied Alice. 'We part to-night. Yes, Redforth,'—for the colonel tucked up his cuffs,—'part to-night! Let us in these next holidays, now going to begin, throw our thoughts into something educational for the grown-up people, hinting to them how things ought to be. Let us veil our meaning under a mask of romance; you, I, and Nettie. William Tinkling being the plainest and quickest writer, shall copy out. Is it agreed?'

The colonel answered sulkily, 'I don't mind.' He then asked, 'How about pretending?'

'We will pretend,' said Alice, 'that we are children; not that we are those grown-up people who won't help us out as they ought, and who understand us so badly.'

The colonel, still much dissatisfied, growled, 'How about waiting?'

'We will wait,' answered little Alice, taking Nettie's hand in hers, and looking up to the sky, 'we will wait—ever constant and true—till the times have got so changed as that everything helps us out, and nothing makes us ridiculous, and the fairies have come back. We will wait—ever constant and true—till we are eighty, ninety, or one hundred. And then the fairies will send *us* children, and we will help them out, poor pretty little creatures, if they pretend ever so much.'

'So we will, dear,' said Nettie Ashford, taking her round the waist with both arms and kissing her. 'And now if my husband will go and buy some cherries for us, I have got some money.'

In the friendliest manner I invited the colonel to go with me; but he so far forgot himself as to acknowledge the invitation by kicking out behind, and then lying down on his stomach on the grass, pulling it up and chewing it. When I came back, however, Alice had nearly brought him out of his vexation, and was soothing him by telling him how soon we should all be ninety.

As we sat under the willow-tree and ate the cherries (fair, for Alice shared them out), we played at being ninety. Nettie complained that she had a bone in her old back, and it made her hobble; and Alice sang a song in an old woman's way, but it was very pretty, and we were all merry. At least, I don't know about merry exactly, but all comfortable.

There was a most tremendous lot of cherries; and Alice always had with her some neat little bag or box or case, to hold things. In it that night was a tiny wine-glass. So Alice and Nettie said they would make some cherry-wine to drink our love at parting.

Each of us had a glassful, and it was delicious; and each of us drank the toast, 'Our love at parting.' The colonel drank his wine last; and it got into my head directly that it got into his directly. Anyhow, his eyes rolled immediately after he had turned the glass upside down; and he took me on one side and proposed in a hoarse whisper, that we should 'Cut 'em out still.'

'How did he mean?' I asked my lawless friend.

'Cut our brides out,' said the colonel, 'and then cut our way, without going down a single turning, bang to the Spanish main!'

We might have tried it, though I didn't think it would answer; only we looked round and saw that there was nothing but moon-light under the willow-tree, and that our pretty, pretty wives were gone. We burst out crying. The colonel gave in second, and came to first; but he gave in strong.

We were ashamed of our red eyes, and hung about for half-an-hour to whiten them. Likewise a piece of chalk round the rims, I doing the colonel's, and he mine, but afterwards found in the bedroom looking-glass not natural, besides inflammation. Our conversation turned on being ninety. The colonel told me he had a pair of boots that wanted soling and heeling; but he thought it hardly worth while to mention it to his father, as he himself should so soon be ninety, when he thought shoes would be more convenient. The colonel also told me, with his hand upon his hip, that he felt himself already getting on in life, and turning rheumatic. And I told him the same. And when they said at our house at supper (they are always bothering about something) that I stooped, I felt so glad!

This is the end of the beginning-part that you were to be-lieve most.

Part II

Romance from the Pen of
Miss Alice Rainbird[2]

---

2.   Aged Seven

THERE was once a king, and he had a queen; and he was the manliest of his sex, and she was the loveliest of hers. The king was, in his private profession, under government. The queen's father had been a medical man out of town.

They had nineteen children, and were always having more. Seventeen of these children took care of the baby; and Alicia, the eldest, took care of them all. Their ages varied from seven years to seven months.

Let us now resume our story.

One day the king was going to the office, when he stopped at the fishmonger's to buy a pound and a half of salmon not too near the tail, which the queen (who was a careful housekeeper) had requested him to send home. Mr. Pickles, the fishmonger, said, 'Certainly, sir; is there any other article? Good-morning.'

The king went on towards the office in a melancholy mood; for quarter-day was such a long way off, and several of the dear children were growing out of their clothes. He had not proceeded far, when Mr. Pickles's errand-boy came running after him, and said, 'Sir, you didn't notice the old lady in our shop.'

'What old lady?' inquired the king. 'I saw none.'

Now the king had not seen any old lady, because this old lady had been invisible to him, though visible to Mr. Pickles's boy. Probably because he messed and splashed the water about to that degree, and flopped the pairs of soles down in that violent manner, that, if she had not been visible to him, he would have spoilt her clothes.

Just then the old lady came trotting up. She was dressed in shot-silk of the richest quality, smelling of dried lavender.

'King Watkins the First, I believe?' said the old lady.

'Watkins,' replied the king, 'is my name.'

'Papa, if I am not mistaken, of the beautiful Princess Alicia?' said the old lady.

'And of eighteen other darlings,' replied the king.

'Listen. You are going to the office,' said the old lady.

It instantly flashed upon the king that she must be a fairy, or how could she know that?

'You are right,' said the old lady, answering his thoughts. 'I am the good Fairy Grandmarina. Attend! When you return home to dinner, politely invite the Princess Alicia to have some of the salmon you bought just now.'

'It may disagree with her,' said the king.

The old lady became so very angry at this absurd idea, that the king was quite alarmed, and humbly begged her pardon.

'We hear a great deal too much about this thing disagreeing, and that thing disagreeing,' said the old lady, with the greatest contempt it was possible to express. 'Don't be greedy. I think you want it all yourself.'

The king hung his head under this reproof, and said he wouldn't talk about things disagreeing any more.

'Be good, then,' said the Fairy Grandmarina, 'and don't. When the beautiful Princess Alicia consents to partake of the salmon,—as I think she will,—you will find she will leave a fish-bone on her plate. Tell her to dry it, and to rub it, and to polish it till it shines like mother-of-pearl, and to take care of it as a present from me.'

'Is that all?' asked the king.

'Don't be impatient, sir,' returned the Fairy Grandmarina, scolding him severely. 'Don't catch people short, before they have done speaking. Just the way with you grown-up persons. You are always doing it.'

The king again hung his head, and said he wouldn't do so any more.

'Be good, then,' said the Fairy Grandmarina, 'and don't! Tell the Princess Alicia, with my love, that the fish-bone is a magic present which can only be used once; but that it will bring her, that once, whatever she wishes for, PROVIDED SHE WISHES FOR IT AT THE RIGHT TIME. That is the message. Take care of it.'

The king was beginning, 'Might I ask the reason?' when the fairy became absolutely furious.

'*Will* you be good, sir?' she exclaimed, stamping her foot on the ground. 'The reason for this, and the reason for that, indeed! You are always wanting the reason. No reason. There! Hoity toity me! I am sick of your grown-up reasons.'

The king was extremely frightened by the old lady's flying into such a passion, and said he was very sorry to have offended her, and he wouldn't ask for reasons any more.

'Be good, then,' said the old lady, 'and don't!'

With those words, Grandmarina vanished, and the king went on and on and on, till he came to the office. There he wrote and wrote and wrote, till it was time to go home again. Then he politely invited the Princess Alicia, as the fairy had directed him, to partake of the salmon. And when she had enjoyed it very much, he saw the fish-bone on her plate, as the fairy had told him he would, and he delivered the fairy's message, and the Princess Alicia took care to dry the bone, and to rub it, and to polish it, till it shone like mother-of-pearl.

And so, when the queen was going to get up in the morning, she said, 'O, dear me, dear me; my head, my head!' and then she fainted away.

The Princess Alicia, who happened to be looking in at the chamber-door, asking about breakfast, was very much alarmed when she saw her royal mamma in this state, and she rang the bell for Peggy, which was the name of the lord chamberlain. But remembering where the smelling-bottle was, she climbed on a chair and got it; and after that she climbed on another chair by the bedside, and held the smelling-bottle to the queen's nose; and after that she jumped down and got some water; and after that she jumped up again and wetted the queen's forehead; and, in short, when the lord chamberlain came in, that dear old woman said to the little princess, 'What a trot you are! I couldn't have done it better myself!'

But that was not the worst of the good queen's illness. O, no! She was very ill indeed, for a long time. The Princess Alicia kept the seventeen young princes and princesses quiet, and dressed and undressed and danced the baby, and made the kettle boil, and heated the soup, and swept the hearth, and poured out the medicine, and nursed the queen, and did all that ever she could, and was as busy, busy, busy as busy could be; for there were not many servants at that palace for three reasons: because the king was short of money, because a rise in his office never seemed to come, and because quarter-day was so far off that it looked almost as far off and as little as one of the stars.

But on the morning when the queen fainted away, where was the magic fish-bone? Why, there it was in the Princess Alicia's pocket! She had almost taken it out to bring the queen to life again, when she put it back, and looked for the smelling-bottle.

After the queen had come out of her swoon that morning, and was dozing, the Princess Alicia hurried up-stairs to tell a most particular secret to a most particularly confidential friend of hers, who was a duchess. People did suppose her to be a doll; but she was really a duchess, though nobody knew it except the princess.

This most particular secret was the secret about the magic fish-bone, the history of which was well known to the duchess, because the princess told her everything. The princess kneeled down by the bed on which the duchess was lying, full-dressed and wide awake, and whispered the secret to her. The duchess smiled and nodded. People might have supposed that she never smiled and nodded; but she often did, though nobody knew it except the princess.

Then the Princess Alicia hurried down-stairs again, to keep watch in the queen's room. She often kept watch by herself in the queen's room; but every evening, while the illness lasted, she sat there watching with the king. And every evening the king sat looking at her with a cross look, wondering why she never brought out the magic fish-bone. As often as she noticed this, she ran up-stairs, whispered the secret to the duchess over again, and said to the duchess besides, 'They think we children never have a reason or a meaning!' And the duchess, though the most fashionable duchess that ever was heard of, winked her eye.

'Alicia,' said the king, one evening, when she wished him good-night.

'Yes, papa.'

'What is become of the magic fish-bone?'

'In my pocket, papa!'

'I thought you had lost it?'

'O, no, papa!'

'Or forgotten it?'

'No, indeed, papa.'

And so another time the dreadful little snapping pug-dog, next door, made a rush at one of the young princes as he stood on the steps coming home from school, and terrified him out of his wits; and he put his hand through a pane of glass, and bled, bled, bled. When the seventeen other young princes and princesses saw him bleed, bleed, bleed, they were terrified out of their wits too, and screamed themselves black in their seventeen faces all at once. But the Princess Alicia put her hands over all their seventeen mouths, one after another, and persuaded them to be quiet because of the sick queen. And then she put the wounded prince's hand in a basin of fresh cold water, while they stared with their twice seventeen are thirty-four, put down four and carry three, eyes, and then she looked in the hand for bits of glass, and there were fortunately no bits of glass there. And then she said to two chubby-legged princes, who were sturdy though small, 'Bring me in the royal rag-bag: I must snip and stitch and cut and contrive.' So these two young princes tugged at the royal rag-bag, and lugged it in; and the Princess Alicia sat down on the floor, with a large pair of scissors and a needle and thread, and snipped and stitched and cut and contrived, and made a bandage, and put it on, and it fitted beautifully; and so when it was all done, she saw the king her papa looking on by the door.

'Alicia.'

'Yes, papa.'

'What have you been doing?'

'Snipping, stitching, cutting, and contriving, papa.'

'Where is the magic fish-bone?'

'In my pocket, papa.'

'I thought you had lost it?'

'O, no, papa.'

'Or forgotten it?'

'No, indeed, papa.'

After that, she ran up-stairs to the duchess, and told her what had passed, and told her the secret over again; and the duchess shook her flaxen curls, and laughed with her rosy lips.

Well! and so another time the baby fell under the grate. The seventeen young princes and princesses were used to it; for they were almost always falling under the grate or down the stairs; but the baby was not used to it yet, and it gave him a swelled face and a black eye. The way the poor little darling came to tumble was, that he was out of the Princess Alicia's lap just as she was sitting, in a great coarse apron that quite smothered her, in front of the kitchen-fire, beginning to peel the turnips for the broth for dinner; and the way she came to be doing that was, that the king's cook had run away that morning with her own true love, who was a very tall but very tipsy soldier. Then the seventeen young princes and princesses, who cried at everything that happened, cried and roared. But the Princess Alicia (who couldn't help crying a little herself) quietly called to them to be still, on account of not throwing back the queen up-stairs, who was fast getting well, and said, 'Hold your tongues, you wicked little monkeys, every one of you, while I examine baby!' Then she examined baby, and found that he hadn't broken anything; and she held cold iron to his poor dear eye, and smoothed his poor dear face, and he presently fell asleep in her arms. Then she said to the seventeen princes and princesses, 'I am afraid to let him down yet, lest he should wake and feel pain; be good, and you shall all be cooks.' They jumped for joy when they heard that, and began making themselves cooks' caps out of old newspapers. So to one she gave the salt-box, and to one she gave the barley, and to one she gave the herbs, and to one she gave the turnips, and to one she gave the carrots, and to one she gave the onions, and to one she gave the spice-box, till they were all cooks, and all running about at work, she sitting in the middle, smothered in the great coarse apron, nursing baby. By and by the broth was done; and the baby woke up, smiling, like an angel, and was trusted to the sedatest princess to hold, while the other princes and princesses were squeezed into a far-off corner to look at the Princess Alicia turning out the saucepanful of broth, for fear (as they were always getting into trouble) they should get splashed and scalded. When the broth came tumbling out, steaming beautifully, and smelling like a nosegay good to eat, they clapped their hands. That made the baby clap his hands; and that, and his looking as if he had a comic toothache, made all the princes and princesses laugh. So the Princess Alicia said, 'Laugh and be good; and after dinner we will make him a nest on the floor in a corner, and he shall sit in his nest and see a dance of eighteen cooks.' That delighted the young princes and princesses, and they ate up all the broth, and washed up all the plates and dishes, and cleared away, and pushed the table into a corner; and then they in their cooks' caps, and the Princess Alicia in the smothering coarse apron that belonged to the cook that had run away with her own true love that was the very tall but very tipsy soldier, danced a dance of eighteen cooks before the angelic baby, who forgot his swelled face and his black eye, and crowed with joy.

And so then, once more the Princess Alicia saw King Watkins the First, her father, standing in the doorway looking on, and he said, 'What have you been doing, Alicia?'

'Cooking and contriving, papa.'

'What else have you been doing, Alicia?'

'Keeping the children light-hearted, papa.'

'Where is the magic fish-bone, Alicia?

'In my pocket, papa.'

'I thought you had lost it?'

'O, no, papa!'

'Or forgotten it?'

'No, indeed, papa.'

The king then sighed so heavily, and seemed so low-spirited, and sat down so miserably, leaning his head upon his hand, and his elbow upon the kitchen-table pushed away in the corner, that the seventeen princes and princesses crept softly out of the kitchen, and left him alone with the Princess Alicia and the angelic baby.

'What is the matter, papa?'

'I am dreadfully poor, my child.'

'Have you no money at all, papa?'

'None, my child.'

'Is there no way of getting any, papa?'

'No way,' said the king. 'I have tried very hard, and I have tried all ways.'

When she heard those last words, the Princess Alicia began to put her hand into the pocket where she kept the magic fish-bone.

'Papa,' said she, 'when we have tried very hard, and tried all ways, we must have done our very, very best?'

'No doubt, Alicia.'

'When we have done our very, very best, papa, and that is not enough, then I think the right time must have come for asking help of others.' This was the very secret connected with the magic fish-bone, which she had found out for herself from the good Fairy Grandmarina's words, and which she had so often whispered to her beautiful and fashionable friend, the duchess.

So she took out of her pocket the magic fish-bone, that had been dried and rubbed and polished till it shone like mother-of-pearl; and she gave it one little kiss, and wished it was quarter-day. And immediately it *was* quarter-day; and the king's quarter's salary came rattling down the chimney, and bounced into the middle of the floor.

But this was not half of what happened,—no, not a quarter; for immediately afterwards the good Fairy Grandmarina came riding in, in a carriage and four (peacocks), with Mr. Pickles's boy up behind, dressed in silver and gold, with a cocked-hat, powdered-hair, pink silk stockings, a jewelled cane, and a nosegay. Down jumped Mr. Pickles's boy, with his cocked-hat in his hand, and wonderfully polite (being entirely changed by enchantment), and handed Grandmarina out; and there she stood, in her rich shot-silk smelling of dried lavender, fanning herself with a sparkling fan.

'Alicia, my dear,' said this charming old fairy, 'how do you do? I hope I see you pretty well? Give me a kiss.'

The Princess Alicia embraced her; and then Grandmarina turned to the king, and said rather sharply, 'Are you good?' The king said he hoped so.

'I suppose you know the reason *now*, why my god-daughter here,' kissing the princess again, 'did not apply to the fish-bone sooner?' said the fairy.

The king made a shy bow.

'Ah! but you didn't *then?*' said the fairy.

The king made a shyer bow.

'Any more reasons to ask for?' said the fairy.

The king said, No, and he was very sorry.

'Be good, then,' said the fairy, 'and live happy ever afterwards.'

Then Grandmarina waved her fan, and the queen came in most splendidly dressed; and the seventeen young princes and princesses, no longer grown out of their clothes, came in, newly fitted out from top to toe, with tucks in everything to admit of its being let out. After that, the fairy tapped the Princess Alicia with her fan; and the smothering coarse apron flew away, and she appeared exquisitely dressed, like a little bride, with a wreath of orange-flowers and a silver veil. After that, the kitchen dresser changed of itself into a wardrobe, made of beautiful woods and gold and looking glass, which was full of dresses of all sorts, all for her and all exactly fitting her. After that, the angelic baby came in, running alone, with his face and eye not a bit the worse, but much the better. Then Grandmarina begged to be introduced to the duchess; and, when the duchess was brought down, many compliments passed between them.

A little whispering took place between the fairy and the duchess; and then the fairy said out loud, 'Yes, I thought she would have told you.' Grandmarina then turned to the king and queen, and said, 'We are going in search of Prince Certainpersonio. The pleasure of your company is requested at church in half an hour precisely.' So she and the Princess Alicia got into the carriage; and Mr. Pickles's boy handed in the duchess, who sat by herself on the opposite seat; and then Mr. Pickles's boy put up the steps and got up behind, and the peacocks flew away with their tails behind.

Prince Certainpersonio was sitting by himself, eating barley-sugar, and waiting to be ninety. When he saw the peacocks, followed by the carriage, coming in at the window it immediately occurred to him that something uncommon was going to happen.

'Prince,' said Grandmarina, 'I bring you your bride.' The moment the fairy said those words, Prince Certainpersonio's face left off being sticky, and his jacket and corduroys changed to peach-bloom velvet, and his hair curled, and a cap and feather flew in like a bird and settled on his head. He got into the carriage by the fairy's invitation; and there he renewed his acquaintance with the duchess, whom he had seen before.

In the church were the prince's relations and friends, and the Princess Alicia's relations and friends, and the seventeen princes and princesses, and the baby, and a crowd of the neighbours. The marriage was beautiful beyond expression. The duchess was bridesmaid, and beheld the ceremony from the pulpit, where she was supported by the cushion of the desk.

Grandmarina gave a magnificent wedding-feast afterwards, in which there was everything and more to eat, and everything and more to drink. The wedding-cake was delicately ornamented with white satin ribbons, frosted silver, and white lilies, and was forty-two yards round.

When Grandmarina had drunk her love to the young couple, and Prince Certainpersonio had made a speech, and everybody had cried, Hip, hip, hip, hurrah! Grandmarina announced to the king and queen that in future there would be eight quarter-days in every year, except in leap-year, when there would be ten. She then turned to Certainpersonio and Alicia, and said, 'My dears, you will have thirty-five children, and they will all be good and beautiful. Seventeen of your children will be boys, and eighteen will be girls. The hair of the whole of your children will curl naturally. They will never have the measles, and will have recovered from the whooping-cough before being born.'

On hearing such good news, everybody cried out 'Hip, hip, hip, hurrah!' again.

'It only remains,' said Grandmarina in conclusion, 'to make an end of the fish-bone.'

So she took it from the hand of the Princess Alicia, and it instantly flew down the throat of the dreadful little snapping pug-dog, next door, and choked him, and he expired in convulsions.

Part III

Romance from the Pen of
Lieut.-Col. Robin Redforth[3]

---

3.   Aged Nine

THE subject of our present narrative would appear to have devoted himself to the pirate profession at a comparatively early age. We find him in command of a splendid schooner of one hundred guns loaded to the muzzle, ere yet he had had a party in honour of his tenth birthday.

It seems that our hero, considering himself spited by a Latin-grammar master, demanded the satisfaction due from one man of honour to another.—Not getting it, he privately withdrew his haughty spirit from such low company, bought a second-hand pocket-pistol, folded up some sandwiches in a paper bag, made a bottle of Spanish liquorice-water, and entered on a career of valour.

It were tedious to follow Boldheart (for such was his name) through the commencing stages of his story. Suffice it, that we find him bearing the rank of Capt. Boldheart, reclining in full uniform on a crimson hearth-rug spread out upon the quarter-deck of his schooner 'The Beauty,' in the China seas. It was a lovely evening; and, as his crew lay grouped about him, he favoured them with the following melody:

> O landsmen are folly!
>
> O pirates are jolly!
>
> O diddleum Dolly,
>
> > Di!
>
> *Chorus.*—Heave yo.

The soothing effect of these animated sounds floating over the waters, as the common sailors united their rough voices to take up the rich tones of Boldheart, may be more easily conceived than described.

It was under these circumstances that the look-out at the masthead gave the word, 'Whales!'

All was now activity.

'Where away?' cried Capt. Boldheart, starting up.

'On the larboard bow, sir,' replied the fellow at the masthead, touching his hat. For such was the height of discipline on board of 'The Beauty,' that, even at that height, he was obliged to mind it, or be shot through the head.

'This adventure belongs to me,' said Boldheart. 'Boy, my harpoon. Let no man follow;' and leaping alone into his boat, the captain rowed with admirable dexterity in the direction of the monster.

All was now excitement.

'He nears him!' said an elderly seaman, following the captain through his spy-glass.

'He strikes him!' said another seaman, a mere stripling, but also with a spy-glass.

'He tows him towards us!' said another seaman, a man in the full vigour of life, but also with a spy-glass.

In fact, the captain was seen approaching, with the huge bulk following. We will not dwell on the deafening cries of 'Boldheart! Boldheart!' with which he was received, when, carelessly leaping on the quarter-deck, he presented his prize to his men. They afterwards made two thousand four hundred and seventeen pound ten and sixpence by it.

Ordering the sail to be braced up, the captain now stood W.N.W. 'The Beauty' flew rather than floated over the dark blue waters. Nothing particular occurred for a fortnight, except taking, with considerable slaughter, four Spanish galleons, and a snow from South America, all richly laden. Inaction began to tell upon the spirits of the men. Capt. Boldheart called all hands aft, and said, 'My lads, I hear there are discontented ones among ye. Let any such stand forth.'

After some murmuring, in which the expressions, 'Ay, ay, sir!' 'Union Jack,' 'Avast,' 'Starboard,' 'Port,' 'Bowsprit,' and similar indications of a mutinous undercurrent, though subdued, were audible, Bill Boozey, captain of the foretop, came out from the rest. His form was that of a giant, but he quailed under the captain's eye.

'What are your wrongs?' said the captain.

'Why, d'ye see, Capt. Boldheart,' replied the towering man-ner, 'I've sailed, man and boy, for many a year, but I never yet know'd the milk served out for the ship's company's teas to be so sour as 'tis aboard this craft.'

At this moment the thrilling cry, 'Man overboard!' an-nounced to the astonished crew that Boozey, in stepping back, as the captain (in mere thoughtfulness) laid his hand upon the faithful pocket-pistol which he wore in his belt, had lost his bal-ance, and was struggling with the foaming tide.

All was now stupefaction.

But with Capt. Boldheart, to throw off his uniform coat, regardless of the various rich orders with which it was decorated, and to plunge into the sea after the drowning giant, was the work of a moment. Maddening was the excitement when boats were lowered; intense the joy when the captain was seen holding up the drowning man with his teeth; deafening the cheering when both were restored to the main deck of 'The Beauty.' And, from the instant of his changing his wet clothes for dry ones, Capt. Boldheart had no such devoted though humble friend as William Boozey.

Boldheart now pointed to the horizon, and called the attention of his crew to the taper spars of a ship lying snug in harbour under the guns of a fort.

'She shall be ours at sunrise,' said he. 'Serve out a double allowance of grog, and prepare for action.'

All was now preparation.

When morning dawned, after a sleepless night, it was seen that the stranger was crowding on all sail to come out of the harbour and offer battle. As the two ships came nearer to each other, the stranger fired a gun and hoisted Roman colours. Boldheart then perceived her to be the Latin-grammar master's bark. Such indeed she was, and had been tacking about the world in unavailing pursuit, from the time of his first taking to a roving life.

Boldheart now addressed his men, promising to blow them up if he should feel convinced that their reputation required it, and giving orders that the Latin-grammar master should be taken alive. He then dismissed them to their quarters, and the fight began with a broadside from 'The Beauty.' She then veered around, and poured in another. 'The Scorpion' (so was the bark of the Latin-grammar master appropriately called) was not slow to return her fire; and a terrific cannonading ensued, in which the guns of 'The Beauty' did tremendous execution.

The Latin-grammar master was seen upon the poop, in the midst of the smoke and fire, encouraging his men. To do him justice, he was no craven, though his white hat, his short gray trousers, and his long snuff-coloured surtout reaching to his heels (the self-same coat in which he had spited Boldheart), contrasted most unfavourably with the brilliant uniform of the latter. At this moment, Boldheart, seizing a pike and putting himself at the head of his men, gave the word to board.

A desperate conflict ensued in the hammock-nettings,—or somewhere in about that direction,—until the Latin-grammar master, having all his masts gone, his hull and rigging shot through, and seeing Boldheart slashing a path towards him, hauled down his flag himself, gave up his sword to Boldheart, and asked for quarter. Scarce had he been put into the captain's boat, ere 'The Scorpion' went down with all on board.

On Capt. Boldheart's now assembling his men, a circumstance occurred. He found it necessary with one blow of his cutlass to kill the cook, who, having lost his brother in the late action, was making at the Latin-grammar master in an infuriated state, intent on his destruction with a carving-knife.

Capt. Boldheart then turned to the Latin-grammar master, severely reproaching him with his perfidy, and put it to his crew what they considered that a master who spited a boy deserved.

They answered with one voice, 'Death.'

'It may be so,' said the captain; 'but it shall never be said that Boldheart stained his hour of triumph with the blood of his enemy. Prepare the cutter.'

The cutter was immediately prepared.

'Without taking your life,' said the captain, 'I must yet for ever deprive you of the power of spiting other boys. I shall turn you adrift in this boat. You will find in her two oars, a compass, a bottle of rum, a small cask of water, a piece of pork, a bag of biscuit, and my Latin grammar. Go! and spite the natives, if you can find any.'

Deeply conscious of this bitter sarcasm, the unhappy wretch was put into the cutter, and was soon left far behind. He made no effort to row, but was seen lying on his back with his legs up, when last made out by the ship's telescopes.

A stiff breeze now beginning to blow, Capt. Boldheart gave orders to keep her S.S.W., easing her a little during the night by falling off a point or two W. by W., or even by W.S., if she complained much. He then retired for the night, having in truth much need of repose. In addition to the fatigues he had undergone, this brave officer had received sixteen wounds in the engagement, but had not mentioned it.

In the morning a white squall came on, and was succeeded by other squalls of various colours. It thundered and lightened heavily for six weeks. Hurricanes then set in for two months. Waterspouts and tornadoes followed. The oldest sailor on board—and he was a very old one—had never seen such weather. 'The Beauty' lost all idea where she was, and the carpenter reported six feet two of water in the hold. Everybody fell senseless at the pumps every day.

Provisions now ran very low. Our hero put the crew on short allowance, and put himself on shorter allowance than any man in the ship. But his spirit kept him fat. In this extremity, the gratitude of Boozey, the captain of the foretop, whom our readers may remember, was truly affecting. The loving though lowly William repeatedly requested to be killed, and preserved for the captain's table.

We now approach a change of affairs. One day during a gleam of sunshine, and when the weather had moderated, the man at the masthead—too weak now to touch his hat, besides its having been blown away—called out,

'Savages!'

All was now expectation.

Presently fifteen hundred canoes, each paddled by twenty savages, were seen advancing in excellent order. They were of a light green colour (the savages were), and sang, with great energy, the following strain:

> *Choo a choo a choo tooth.*
> *Muntch, muntch. Nycey!*
> *Choo a choo a choo tooth.*
> *Muntch, muntch. Nycey!*

As the shades of night were by this time closing in, these expressions were supposed to embody this simple people's views of the evening hymn. But it too soon appeared that the song was a translation of 'For what we are going to receive,' &c.

The chief, imposingly decorated with feathers of lively colours, and having the majestic appearance of a fighting parrot, no sooner understood (he understood English perfectly) that the ship was 'The Beauty,' Capt. Boldheart, than he fell upon his face on the deck, and could not be persuaded to rise until the captain had lifted him up, and told him he wouldn't hurt him. All the rest of the savages also fell on their faces with marks of terror, and had also to be lifted up one by one. Thus the fame of the great Boldheart had gone before him, even among these children of Nature.

Turtles and oysters were now produced in astonishing numbers; and on these and yams the people made a hearty meal. After dinner the chief told Capt. Boldheart that there was better feeding up at the village, and that he would be glad to take him and his officers there. Apprehensive of treachery, Boldheart ordered his boat's crew to attend him completely armed. And well were it for other commanders if their precautions—but let us not anticipate.

When the canoes arrived at the beach, the darkness of the night was illumined by the light of an immense fire. Ordering his boat's crew (with the intrepid though illiterate William at their head) to keep close and be upon their guard, Boldheart bravely went on, arm in arm with the chief.

But how to depict the captain's surprise when he found a ring of savages singing in chorus that barbarous translation of 'For what we are going to receive,' &c., which has been given above, and dancing hand in hand round the Latin-grammar master, in a hamper with his head shaved, while two savages floured him, before putting him to the fire to be cooked!

Boldheart now took counsel with his officers on the course to be adopted. In the mean time, the miserable captive never ceased begging pardon and imploring to be delivered. On the generous Boldheart's proposal, it was at length resolved that he should not be cooked, but should be allowed to remain raw, on two conditions, namely:

1. That he should never, under any circumstances, presume to teach any boy anything any more.

2. That, if taken back to England, he should pass his life in travelling to find out boys who wanted their exercises done, and should do their exercises for those boys for nothing, and never say a word about it.

Drawing the sword from its sheath, Boldheart swore him to these conditions on its shining blade. The prisoner wept bitterly, and appeared acutely to feel the errors of his past career.

The captain then ordered his boat's crew to make ready for a volley, and after firing to re-load quickly. 'And expect a score or two on ye to go head over heels,' murmured William Boozey; 'for I'm a-looking at ye.' With those words, the derisive though deadly William took a good aim.

'Fire!'

The ringing voice of Boldheart was lost in the report of the guns and the screeching of the savages. Volley after volley awakened the numerous echoes. Hundreds of savages were killed, hundreds wounded, and thousands ran howling into the woods. The Latin-grammar master had a spare night-cap lent him, and a long-tail coat, which he wore hind side before. He presented a ludicrous though pitiable appearance, and serve him right.

We now find Capt. Boldheart, with this rescued wretch on board, standing off for other islands. At one of these, not a cannibal island, but a pork and vegetable one, he married (only in fun on his part) the king's daughter. Here he rested some time, receiving from the natives great quantities of precious stones, gold dust, elephants' teeth, and sandal wood, and getting very rich. This, too, though he almost every day made presents of enormous value to his men.

The ship being at length as full as she could hold of all sorts of valuable things, Boldheart gave orders to weigh the anchor, and turn 'The Beauty's' head towards England. These orders were obeyed with three cheers; and ere the sun went down full many a hornpipe had been danced on deck by the uncouth though agile William.

We next find Capt. Boldheart about three leagues off Madeira, surveying through his spy-glass a stranger of suspicious appearance making sail towards him. On his firing a gun ahead of her to bring her to, she ran up a flag, which he instantly recognised as the flag from the mast in the back-garden at home.

Inferring from this, that his father had put to sea to seek his long-lost son, the captain sent his own boat on board the stranger to inquire if this was so, and, if so, whether his father's intentions were strictly honourable. The boat came back with a present of greens and fresh meat, and reported that the stranger was 'The Family,' of twelve hundred tons, and had not only the captain's father on board, but also his mother, with the majority of his aunts and uncles, and all his cousins. It was further reported to Boldheart that the whole of these relations had expressed themselves in a becoming manner, and were anxious to embrace him and thank him for the glorious credit he had done them. Boldheart at once invited them to breakfast next morning on board 'The Beauty,' and gave orders for a brilliant ball that should last all day.

It was in the course of the night that the captain discovered the hopelessness of reclaiming the Latin-grammar master. That thankless traitor was found out, as the two ships lay near each other, communicating with 'The Family' by signals, and offering to give up Boldheart. He was hanged at the yard-arm the first thing in the morning, after having it impressively pointed out to him by Boldheart that this was what spiters came to.

The meeting between the captain and his parents was attended with tears. His uncles and aunts would have attended their meeting with tears too, but he wasn't going to stand that. His cousins were very much astonished by the size of his ship and the discipline of his men, and were greatly overcome by the splendour of his uniform. He kindly conducted them round the vessel, and pointed out everything worthy of notice. He also fired his hundred guns, and found it amusing to witness their alarm.

The entertainment surpassed everything ever seen on board ship, and lasted from ten in the morning until seven the next morning. Only one disagreeable incident occurred. Capt. Boldheart found himself obliged to put his cousin Tom in irons, for being disrespectful. On the boy's promising amendment, however, he was humanely released after a few hours' close confinement.

Boldheart now took his mother down into the great cabin, and asked after the young lady with whom, it was well known to the world, he was in love. His mother replied that the object of his affections was then at school at Margate, for the benefit of sea-bathing (it was the month of September), but that she feared the young lady's friends were still opposed to the union. Boldheart at once resolved, if necessary, to bombard the town.

Taking the command of his ship with this intention, and putting all but fighting men on board 'The Family,' with orders to that vessel to keep in company, Boldheart soon anchored in Margate Roads. Here he went ashore well-armed, and attended by his boat's crew (at their head the faithful though ferocious William), and demanded to see the mayor, who came out of his office.

'Dost know the name of yon ship, mayor?' asked Boldheart fiercely.

'No,' said the mayor, rubbing his eyes, which he could scarce believe, when he saw the goodly vessel riding at anchor.

'She is named "The Beauty,"' said the captain.

'Hah!' exclaimed the mayor, with a start. 'And you, then, are Capt. Boldheart?'

'The same.'

A pause ensued. The mayor trembled.

'Now, mayor,' said the captain, 'choose! Help me to my bride, or be bombarded.'

The mayor begged for two hours' grace, in which to make inquiries respecting the young lady. Boldheart accorded him but one; and during that one placed William Boozey sentry over him, with a drawn sword, and instructions to accompany him wherever he went, and to run him through the body if he showed a sign of playing false.

At the end of the hour the mayor re-appeared more dead than alive, closely waited on by Boozey more alive than dead.

'Captain,' said the mayor, 'I have ascertained that the young lady is going to bathe. Even now she waits her turn for a machine. The tide is low, though rising. I, in one of our town-boats, shall not be suspected. When she comes forth in her bathing-dress into the shallow water from behind the hood of the machine, my boat shall intercept her and prevent her return. Do you the rest.'

'Mayor,' returned Capt. Boldheart, 'thou hast saved thy town.'

The captain then signalled his boat to take him off, and, steering her himself, ordered her crew to row towards the bathing-ground, and there to rest upon their oars. All happened as had been arranged. His lovely bride came forth, the mayor glided in behind her, she became confused, and had floated out of her depth, when, with one skilful touch of the rudder and one quivering stroke from the boat's crew, her adoring Boldheart held her in his strong arms. There her shrieks of terror were changed to cries of joy.

Before 'The Beauty' could get under way, the hoisting of all the flags in the town and harbour, and the ringing of all the bells, announced to the brave Boldheart that he had nothing to fear. He therefore determined to be married on the spot, and signalled for a clergyman and clerk, who came off promptly in a sailing-boat named 'The Skylark.' Another great entertainment was then given on board 'The Beauty,' in the midst of which the mayor was called out by a messenger. He returned with the news that government had sent down to know whether Capt.

Boldheart, in acknowledgment of the great services he had done his country by being a pirate, would consent to be made a lieutenant-colonel. For himself he would have spurned the worthless boon; but his bride wished it, and he consented.

Only one thing further happened before the good ship 'Family' was dismissed, with rich presents to all on board. It is painful to record (but such is human nature in some cousins) that Capt. Boldheart's unmannerly Cousin Tom was actually tied up to receive three dozen with a rope's end 'for cheekiness and making game,' when Capt. Boldheart's lady begged for him, and he was spared. 'The Beauty' then refitted, and the captain and his bride departed for the Indian Ocean to enjoy themselves for evermore.

Part IV

Romance from the Pen of
Miss Nettie Ashford[4]

---

4.   Aged half-past six.

THERE is a country, which I will show you when I get into maps, where the children have everything their own way. It is a most delightful country to live in. The grown-up people are obliged to obey the children, and are never allowed to sit up to supper, except on their birthdays. The children order them to make jam and jelly and marmalade, and tarts and pies and puddings, and all manner of pastry. If they say they won't, they are put in the corner till they do. They are sometimes allowed to have some; but when they have some, they generally have powders given them afterwards.

One of the inhabitants of this country, a truly sweet young creature of the name of Mrs. Orange, had the misfortune to be sadly plagued by her numerous family. Her parents required a great deal of looking after, and they had connections and companions who were scarcely ever out of mischief. So Mrs. Orange said to herself, 'I really cannot be troubled with these torments any longer: I must put them all to school.'

Mrs. Orange took off her pinafore, and dressed herself very nicely, and took up her baby, and went out to call upon another lady of the name of Mrs. Lemon, who kept a preparatory establishment. Mrs. Orange stood upon the scraper to pull at the bell, and give a ring-ting-ting.

Mrs. Lemon's neat little housemaid, pulling up her socks as she came along the passage, answered the ring-ting-ting.

'Good-morning,' said Mrs. Orange. 'Fine day. How do you do? Mrs. Lemon at home!'

'Yes, ma'am.'

'Will you say Mrs. Orange and baby?'

'Yes, ma'am. Walk in.'

Mrs. Orange's baby was a very fine one, and real wax all over. Mrs. Lemon's baby was leather and bran. However, when Mrs. Lemon came into the drawing-room with her baby in her arms, Mrs. Orange said politely, 'Good-morning. Fine day. How do you do? And how is little Tootleumboots?'

'Well, she is but poorly. Cutting her teeth, ma'am,' said Mrs. Lemon.

'O, indeed, ma'am!' said Mrs. Orange. 'No fits, I hope?'

'No, ma'am.'

'How many teeth has she, ma'am?'

'Five, ma'am.'

'My Emilia, ma'am, has eight,' said Mrs. Orange. 'Shall we lay them on the mantelpiece side by side, while we converse?'

'By all means, ma'am,' said Mrs. Lemon. 'Hem!'

'The first question is, ma'am,' said Mrs. Orange, 'I don't bore you?'

'Not in the least, ma'am,' said Mrs. Lemon. 'Far from it, I assure you.'

'Then pray *have* you,' said Mrs. Orange,—'*have* you any vacancies?'

'Yes, ma'am. How many might you require?'

'Why, the truth is, ma'am,' said Mrs. Orange, 'I have come to the conclusion that my children,'—O, I forgot to say that they call the grown-up people children in that country!—'that my children are getting positively too much for me. Let me see. Two parents, two intimate friends of theirs, one godfather, two godmothers, and an aunt. *Have* you as many as eight vacancies?'

'I have just eight, ma'am,' said Mrs. Lemon.

'Most fortunate! Terms moderate, I think?'

'Very moderate, ma'am.'

'Diet good, I believe?'

'Excellent, ma'am.'

'Unlimited?'

'Unlimited.'

'Most satisfactory! Corporal punishment dispensed with?'

'Why, we do occasionally shake,' said Mrs. Lemon, 'and we have slapped. But only in extreme cases.'

'*Could* I, ma'am,' said Mrs. Orange,—'*could* I see the establishment?'

'With the greatest of pleasure, ma'am,' said Mrs. Lemon.

Mrs. Lemon took Mrs. Orange into the schoolroom, where there were a number of pupils. 'Stand up, children,' said Mrs. Lemon; and they all stood up.

Mrs. Orange whispered to Mrs. Lemon, 'There is a pale, bald child, with red whiskers, in disgrace. Might I ask what he has done?'

'Come here, White,' said Mrs. Lemon, 'and tell this lady what you have been doing.'

'Betting on horses,' said White sulkily.

'Are you sorry for it, you naughty child?' said Mrs. Lemon.

'No,' said White. 'Sorry to lose, but shouldn't be sorry to win.'

'There's a vicious boy for you, ma'am,' said Mrs. Lemon. 'Go along with you, sir. This is Brown, Mrs. Orange. O, a sad case, Brown's! Never knows when he has had enough. Greedy. How is your gout, sir?'

'Bad,' said Brown.

'What else can you expect?' said Mrs. Lemon. 'Your stomach is the size of two. Go and take exercise directly. Mrs. Black, come here to me. Now, here is a child, Mrs. Orange, ma'am, who is always at play. She can't be kept at home a single day together; always gadding about and spoiling her clothes. Play, play, play, play, from morning to night, and to morning again. How can she expect to improve?'

'Don't expect to improve,' sulked Mrs. Black. 'Don't want to.'

'There is a specimen of her temper, ma'am,' said Mrs. Lemon. 'To see her when she is tearing about, neglecting everything else, you would suppose her to be at least good-humoured. But bless you! ma'am, she is as pert and flouncing a minx as ever you met with in all your days!'

'You must have a great deal of trouble with them, ma'am,' said Mrs. Orange.

'Ah, I have, indeed, ma'am!' said Mrs. Lemon. 'What with their tempers, what with their quarrels, what with their never knowing what's good for them, and what with their always wanting to domineer, deliver me from these unreasonable children!'

'Well, I wish you good-morning, ma'am,' said Mrs. Orange.

'Well, I wish you good-morning, ma'am,' said Mrs. Lemon.

So Mrs. Orange took up her baby and went home, and told the family that plagued her so that they were all going to be sent to school. They said they didn't want to go to school; but she packed up their boxes, and packed them off.

'O dear me, dear me! Rest and be thankful!' said Mrs. Orange, throwing herself back in her little arm-chair. 'Those troublesome troubles are got rid of, please the pigs!'

Just then another lady, named Mrs. Alicumpaine, came calling at the street-door with a ring-ting-ting.

'My dear Mrs. Alicumpaine,' said Mrs. Orange, 'how do you do? Pray stay to dinner. We have but a simple joint of sweet-stuff, followed by a plain dish of bread and treacle; but, if you will take us as you find us, it will be *so* kind!'

'Don't mention it,' said Mrs. Alicumpaine. 'I shall be too glad. But what do you think I have come for, ma'am? Guess, ma'am.'

'I really cannot guess, ma'am,' said Mrs. Orange.

'Why, I am going to have a small juvenile party to-night,' said Mrs. Alicumpaine; 'and if you and Mr. Orange and baby would but join us, we should be complete.'

'More than charmed, I am sure!' said Mrs. Orange.

'So kind of you!' said Mrs. Alicumpaine. 'But I hope the children won't bore you?'

'Dear things! Not at all,' said Mrs. Orange. 'I dote upon them.'

Mr. Orange here came home from the city; and he came, too, with a ring-ting-ting.

'James love,' said Mrs. Orange, 'you look tired. What has been doing in the city to-day?'

'Trap, bat, and ball, my dear,' said Mr. Orange, 'and it knocks a man up.'

'That dreadfully anxious city, ma'am,' said Mrs. Orange to Mrs. Alicumpaine; 'so wearing, is it not?'

'O, so trying!' said Mrs. Alicumpaine. 'John has lately been speculating in the peg-top ring; and I often say to him at night, "John, *is* the result worth the wear and tear?"'

Dinner was ready by this time: so they sat down to dinner; and while Mr. Orange carved the joint of sweet-stuff, he said, 'It's a poor heart that never rejoices. Jane, go down to the cellar, and fetch a bottle of the Upest ginger-beer.'

At tea-time, Mr. and Mrs. Orange, and baby, and Mrs. Alicumpaine went off to Mrs. Alicumpaine's house. The children had not come yet; but the ball-room was ready for them, decorated with paper flowers.

'How very sweet!' said Mrs. Orange. 'The dear things! How pleased they will be!'

'I don't care for children myself,' said Mr. Orange, gaping.

'Not for girls?' said Mrs. Alicumpaine. 'Come! you care for girls?'

Mr. Orange shook his head, and gaped again. 'Frivolous and vain, ma'am.'

'My dear James,' cried Mrs. Orange, who had been peeping about, 'do look here. Here's the supper for the darlings, ready laid in the room behind the folding-doors. Here's their little pickled salmon, I do declare! And here's their little salad, and their little roast beef and fowls, and their little pastry, and their wee, wee, wee champagne!'

'Yes, I thought it best, ma'am,' said Mrs. Alicumpaine, 'that they should have their supper by themselves. Our table is in the corner here, where the gentlemen can have their wineglass of negus, and their egg-sandwich, and their quiet game at beggar-my-neighbour, and look on. As for us, ma'am, we shall have quite enough to do to manage the company.'

'O, indeed, you may say so! Quite enough, ma'am,' said Mrs. Orange.

The company began to come. The first of them was a stout boy, with a white top-knot and spectacles. The housemaid brought him in and said, 'Compliments, and at what time was he to be fetched!' Mrs. Alicumpaine said, 'Not a moment later than ten. How do you do, sir? Go and sit down.' Then a number of other children came; boys by themselves, and girls by themselves, and boys and girls together. They didn't behave at all well. Some of them looked through quizzing-glasses at others, and said, 'Who are those? Don't know them.' Some of them looked through quizzing-glasses at others, and said, 'How do?' Some of them had cups of tea or coffee handed to them by others, and said, 'Thanks; much!' A good many boys stood about, and felt their shirt-collars. Four tiresome fat boys *would* stand in the doorway, and talk about the newspapers, till Mrs. Alicumpaine went to them and said, 'My dears, I really cannot allow you to prevent people from coming in. I shall be truly sorry to do it; but, if you put yourself in everybody's way, I must positively send you home.' One boy, with a beard and a large white waistcoat, who stood straddling on the hearth-rug warming his coat-tails, *was* sent home. 'Highly incorrect, my dear,' said Mrs. Alicumpaine, handing him out of the room, 'and I cannot permit it.'

There was a children's band,—harp, cornet, and piano,—and Mrs. Alicumpaine and Mrs. Orange bustled among the children to persuade them to take partners and dance. But they were so obstinate! For quite a long time they would not be persuaded to take partners and dance. Most of the boys said, 'Thanks; much! But not at present.' And most of the rest of the boys said, 'Thanks; much! But never do.'

'O, these children are very wearing!' said Mrs. Alicumpaine to Mrs. Orange.

'Dear things! I dote upon them; but they ARE wearing,' said Mrs. Orange to Mrs. Alicumpaine.

At last they did begin in a slow and melancholy way to slide about to the music; though even then they wouldn't mind what they were told, but would have this partner, and wouldn't have that partner, and showed temper about it. And they wouldn't smile,—no, not on any account they wouldn't; but, when the music stopped, went round and round the room in dismal twos, as if everybody else was dead.

'O, it's very hard indeed to get these vexing children to be entertained!' said Mrs. Alicumpaine to Mrs. Orange.

'I dote upon the darlings; but it is hard,' said Mrs. Orange to Mrs. Alicumpaine.

They were trying children, that's the truth. First, they wouldn't sing when they were asked; and then, when everybody fully believed they wouldn't, they would. 'If you serve us so any more, my love,' said Mrs. Alicumpaine to a tall child, with a good deal of white back, in mauve silk trimmed with lace, 'it will be my painful privilege to offer you a bed, and to send you to it immediately.'

The girls were so ridiculously dressed, too, that they were in rags before supper. How could the boys help treading on their trains? And yet when their trains were trodden on, they often showed temper again, and looked as black, they did! However, they all seemed to be pleased when Mrs. Alicumpaine said, 'Supper is ready, children!' And they went crowding and pushing in, as if they had had dry bread for dinner.

'How are the children getting on?' said Mr. Orange to Mrs. Orange, when Mrs. Orange came to look after baby. Mrs. Orange had left baby on a shelf near Mr. Orange while he played at beggar-my-neighbour, and had asked him to keep his eye upon her now and then.

'Most charmingly, my dear!' said Mrs. Orange. 'So droll to see their little flirtations and jealousies! Do come and look!'

'Much obliged to you, my dear,' said Mr. Orange; 'but I don't care about children myself.'

So Mrs. Orange, having seen that baby was safe, went back without Mr. Orange to the room where the children were having supper.

'What are they doing now?' said Mrs. Orange to Mrs. Alicumpaine.

'They are making speeches, and playing at parliament,' said Mrs. Alicumpaine to Mrs. Orange.

On hearing this, Mrs. Orange set off once more back again to Mr. Orange, and said, 'James dear, do come. The children are playing at parliament.'

'Thank you, my dear,' said Mr. Orange, 'but I don't care about parliament myself.'

So Mrs. Orange went once again without Mr. Orange to the room where the children were having supper, to see them playing at parliament. And she found some of the boys crying, 'Hear, hear, hear!' while other boys cried 'No, no!' and others, 'Question!' 'Spoke!' and all sorts of nonsense that ever you heard. Then one of those tiresome fat boys who had stopped the doorway told them he was on his legs (as if they couldn't see that he wasn't on his head, or on his anything else) to explain, and that, with the permission of his honourable friend, if he would allow him to call him so (another tiresome boy bowed), he would proceed to explain. Then he went on for a long time in a sing-song (whatever he meant), did this troublesome fat boy, about that he held in his hand a glass; and about that he had come down to that house that night to discharge what he would call a public duty; and about that, on the present occasion, he would lay his hand (his other hand) upon his heart, and would tell honourable gentlemen that he was about to open the door to general approval. Then he opened the door by saying, 'To our hostess!' and everybody else said 'To our hostess!' and then there were cheers. Then another tiresome boy started up in sing-song, and then half a dozen noisy and nonsensical boys at once. But at last Mrs. Alicumpaine said, 'I cannot have this din. Now, children, you have played at parliament very nicely; but parliament gets tiresome after a little while, and it's time you left off, for you will soon be fetched.'

After another dance (with more tearing to rags than before supper), they began to be fetched; and you will be very glad to be told that the tiresome fat boy who had been on his legs was walked off first without any ceremony. When they were all gone, poor Mrs. Alicumpaine dropped upon a sofa, and said to Mrs. Orange, 'These children will be the death of me at last, ma'am,— they will indeed!'

'I quite adore them, ma'am,' said Mrs. Orange; 'but they DO want variety.'

Mr. Orange got his hat, and Mrs. Orange got her bonnet and her baby, and they set out to walk home. They had to pass Mrs. Lemon's preparatory establishment on their way.

'I wonder, James dear,' said Mrs. Orange, looking up at the window, 'whether the precious children are asleep!'

'I don't care much whether they are or not, myself,' said Mr. Orange.

'James dear!'

'You dote upon them, you know,' said Mr. Orange. 'That's another thing.'

'I do,' said Mrs. Orange rapturously. 'O, I DO!'

'I don't,' said Mr. Orange.

'But I was thinking, James love,' said Mrs. Orange, pressing his arm, 'whether our dear, good, kind Mrs. Lemon would like them to stay the holidays with her.'

'If she was paid for it, I daresay she would,' said Mr. Orange.

'I adore them, James,' said Mrs. Orange, 'but SUPPOSE we pay her, then!'

This was what brought that country to such perfection, and made it such a delightful place to live in. The grown-up people (that would be in other countries) soon left off being allowed any holidays after Mr. and Mrs. Orange tried the experiment; and the children (that would be in other countries) kept them at school as long as ever they lived, and made them do whatever they were told.

Made in the USA
Monee, IL
07 July 2026